JOURNEY TO THE RIVER SEA

DINOSAUR COVE™

Other books in the series:

LATE CRETACEOUS

Attack of the
LIZARD KING

Charge of the
THREE-HORNED MONSTER

March of the
ARMOURED BEASTS

Flight of the
WINGED SERPENT

Catching the
SPEEDY THIEF

Stampede of the
GIANT REPTILES

JURASSIC

Rescuing the
PLATED LIZARD

Swimming with the
SEA MONSTER

Tracking the
GIGANTIC BEAST

Finding the
DECEPTIVE DINOSAUR

Escape from the
FIERCE PREDATOR

Assault of the
FRIENDLY FIENDS

DINOSAUR COVE™

JOURNEY TO THE ICE AGE

by
REX STONE

illustrated by
MIKE SPOOR

Series created by
Working Partners Ltd

OXFORD
UNIVERSITY PRESS

Special thanks to Jane Clarke

To Barbara and Annette, and library friends
everywhere – R.S.

The illustrations in this book are dedicated to Karen Stewart
for her unlimited enthusiasm and guidance – M.S.

OXFORD
UNIVERSITY PRESS

Great Clarendon Street, Oxford OX2 6DP
Oxford University Press is a department of the University of Oxford.
It furthers the University's objective of excellence in research, scholarship,
and education by publishing worldwide in

Oxford   New York

Auckland   Cape Town   Dar es Salaam   Hong Kong   Karachi
Kuala Lumpur   Madrid   Melbourne   Mexico City   Nairobi
New Delhi   Shanghai   Taipei   Toronto

With offices in

Argentina   Austria   Brazil   Chile   Czech Republic   France   Greece
Guatemala   Hungary   Italy   Japan   Poland   Portugal   Singapore
South Korea   Switzerland   Thailand   Turkey   Ukraine   Vietnam

Oxford is a registered trade mark of Oxford University Press
in the UK and in certain other countries

British Library Cataloguing in Publication Data

Data available

ISBN: 978-0-19-272927-9

1 3 5 7 9 10 8 6 4 2

Printed in Great Britain by CPI Cox and Wyman, Reading, Berkshire
Paper used in the production of this book is a natural,
recyclable product made from wood grown in sustainable forests
The manufacturing process conforms to the environmental
regulations of the country of origin

FACT FILE

➡️ JAMIE'S DAD'S MUSEUM ON THE BOTTOM FLOOR OF THE LIGHTHOUSE IN DINOSAUR COVE IS THE SECOND BEST PLACE IN THE WORLD TO BE. THE FIRST IS DINO WORLD, OF COURSE, THE SECRET THAT JAMIE AND HIS BEST FRIEND TOM HAVE DISCOVERED IN THE BACK OF A DEEP, DARK CAVE. THE BOYS HAVE MET ALL KINDS OF DINOSAURS, BUT THIS TIME THEIR ADVENTURE IS A LITTLE BIT HAIRIER.

JAMIE

- **FULL NAME:** JAMIE MORGAN
- **AGE:** 8 YEARS
- **SIZE:** 1 JATOM*
- **TOP SPEED:** 10 KPH
- **LIKES:** FOSSIL HUNTING AND LEARNING ABOUT DINOSAURS
- **DISLIKES:** BEING STUCK INDOORS

Jamie's eye

Jamie's foot

Jamie's hand

*NOTE: A JATOM IS THE SIZE OF JAMIE OR TOM: 125 CM TALL AND 27 KG IN WEIGHT

TOM

- **FULL NAME:** THOMAS CLAY
- **AGE:** 8 YEARS
- **SIZE:** 1 JATOM*
- **TOP SPEED:** 10 KPH
- **LIKES:** TRACKING ANIMALS AND EXPLORING WILDLIFE
- **DISLIKES:** RAINY DAYS

Tom's eye   Tom's hand

WANNA

- **FULL NAME:** WANNANOSAURUS
- **AGE:** 65 – 80 MILLION YEARS**
- **SIZE:** LESS THAN A JATOM*
- **TOP SPEED:** 50 KPH, ESPECIALLY WHEN BEING CHASED BY A T-REX
- **LIKES:** STINKY GINGKO FRUIT AND BANGING HIS HEAD ON TREE TRUNKS
- **DISLIKES:** SCARY DINOSAURS

Wanna's head   Wanna's foot

*NOTE: A JATOM IS THE SIZE OF JAMIE OR TOM: 125 CM TALL AND 27 KG IN WEIGHT
**NOTE: SCIENTISTS CALL THIS PERIOD THE LATE CRETACEOUS

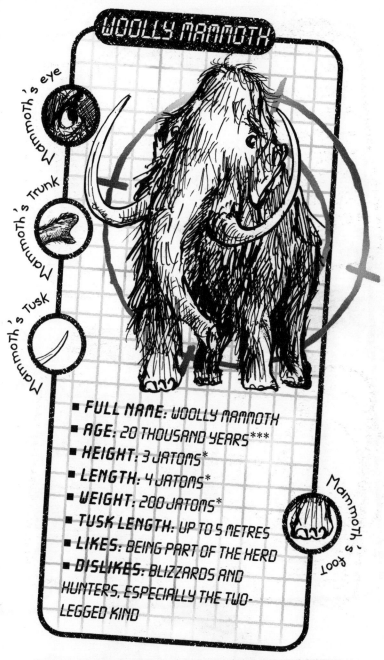

WOOLLY MAMMOTH

Mammoth's eye

Mammoth's Trunk

Mammoth's Tusk

Mammoth's foot

- **FULL NAME:** WOOLLY MAMMOTH
- **AGE:** 20 THOUSAND YEARS***
- **HEIGHT:** 3 JATOMS*
- **LENGTH:** 4 JATOMS*
- **WEIGHT:** 200 JATOMS*
- **TUSK LENGTH:** UP TO 5 METRES
- **LIKES:** BEING PART OF THE HERD
- **DISLIKES:** BLIZZARDS AND HUNTERS, ESPECIALLY THE TWO-LEGGED KIND

*NOTE: A JATOM IS THE SIZE OF JAMIE OR TOM: 125 CM TALL AND 27 KG IN WEIGHT
***NOTE: THIS PERIOD IS PART OF THE ICE AGE

DINOSAUR COVE

Village

Marina

Sealight Hea'

8

Landslips where
clay and fossils are

DINO CAVE

High Tide beach line

Low Tide beach line

Muddy beach

Smuggler's Point

Sea

9

CHAPTER 1

Jamie Morgan laughed as his best friend Tom Clay perched a red Santa hat on the bony skull of a stegosaurus.

It was Christmas Eve in Dinosaur Cove, and Jamie's dad's dinosaur museum in the old lighthouse sparkled with red and gold Christmas decorations. The huge edmontosaurus skeleton looked as if it was about to nibble the star on top of the enormous Christmas tree.

11

'What do you call a T-Rex in a
Santa hat?' Tom joked.

'What?' Jamie asked.

'Santa Jaws!' Tom declared.

Jamie snorted. 'I wouldn't
want him coming down
the chimney!'

'He'd eat all the mince
pies,' Tom said. 'And the
reindeer!' The boys fell
about laughing.

12

'Great decorations,' Jamie's grandad said as he stuck his head into the room. 'Perfect for our dinosaur Christmas party this evening. And we just finished the Ice Age exhibition. Come and see.'

The boys followed Grandad into an artificial snow cave dripping with fake icicles in the corner of the museum. On the back wall, there was a movie screen showing a river of blue-grey ice moving slowly down a snowy mountainside.

'That's a speeded up glacier,' Jamie's dad explained. 'Twenty thousand years ago, there were glaciers all over northern Europe and America.'

'Brrr!' Tom said. 'It must have been cold.'

'It was the Ice Age, you wombat.' Jamie grinned. 'What are these, Dad?' He pointed

to two fossils in a case. They looked a bit like upside-down trainers with deeply ridged soles.

'Teeth from a woolly mammoth,' his dad said.

'Awesome!' Tom said. 'Mammoths were even bigger than elephants.'

'That's right, and they lived on frozen land called tundra,' Jamie's dad went on. 'Early humans followed herds of mammoths and hunted them with weapons like this.' He showed them a replica wooden spear with a tip made of a sharpened antler.

'People were nomads then, searching out the best places to hunt and gather what they needed. I wonder what it was like . . . ' Dad gazed at the worked flint axe heads with a faraway look.

'I've been hunter-gathering,' Grandad said, with a twinkle in his eye. 'I call it Christmas shopping.'

He pressed what looked like a ball of silver tape into Tom's hand. 'Here, my boy. Merry Christmas!'

'Wow, thanks!' Tom's eyes lit up. 'Can I open it now?'

'You can't open a Christmas present before Christmas,' Jamie said.

'OK, OK.' Tom reluctantly stuffed his gift into his pocket. 'I'll open it tomorrow.'

'We should get back to work,' Dad said, straightening the Ice Age brochures on the display table. 'Lots to do before the party tonight.'

'And lots of presents to wrap before tomorrow.' Grandad winked at Jamie and followed Dad out of the ice cave.

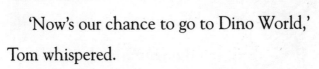

'Now's our chance to go to Dino World,' Tom whispered.

Jamie glanced round to make sure his dad and grandad hadn't overheard. No one

knew about the secret
cave that he and Tom
had discovered in
Dinosaur Cove. The
cave led to Dino
World, a world of
living, breathing
prehistoric creatures,
where Wanna, their little
dinosaur friend, was always
waiting for their next visit.

'I can't wait to give Wanna his present,'

Jamie thought. The boys planned to pick Wanna a feast of stinky gingko fruit for Christmas.

'We're off exploring,' Jamie announced as he grabbed his backpack and headed for the door.

'Wait! You need coats.' Jamie's dad fetched their coats, woolly socks, and gloves. He stood by as the boys put them on.

'Hang on, me hearties.' Grandad disappeared into the kitchen and returned with a couple of foil-wrapped packages. 'Cheese and pickle sandwiches for you, and a slab of birdseed cake. That's my Christmas present to the local wildlife.'

'Thanks, Grandad,' Jamie said as he shoved the supplies into his backpack.

19

Outside, the sky was
the colour of grey slate.
An icy wind blew Jamie
and Tom along the path
towards Smuggler's Point.

Jamie was glad of his warm coat.

'I hope it snows for Christmas,' Tom said, as they scrambled up and over the rocks.

'That'd be awesome!' Jamie took out his torch, and they headed for the back of the cave and squeezed through the gap into the secret cave beyond. It felt even colder inside the cave than it did outside.

'I'm keeping my coat on.' Jamie shivered as he fitted his left foot into the first fossil dinosaur footprint that led across the cave floor.

'I can't wait to get into the steamy j-j-jungle in D-D-Dino World.' Tom was close behind him, with his teeth chattering.

'Here we go. One . . . two . . . **three** . . . **four** . . . ' Jamie counted the footsteps as they stepped towards the rock face.

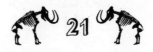

21

'Five...'

There was a blinding flash of light and suddenly Jamie's foot slipped from under him and he crash-landed on his knee. 'Ouch!' he yelled.

'Owww!' Tom slammed into him.

Jamie picked himself up from the hard cold ground and looked around. 'How strange!' he said. 'Wanna's footprints have turned to ice.' The shallow cave was edged with sparkling icicles.

Outside the cave there was ice and
snow everywhere, twinkling in the
wintry sunshine.

'Wow. It's Christmas here, too,'
Tom said. 'We've never seen Dino World
like this before!'

'Where are we?' A bitter cold wind blew Jamie's steamy breath away as he walked out of the cave. 'This doesn't seem like the Jurassic.'

'We're halfway up a mountain,' Tom said, stepping carefully into the snow. 'But where's the jungle? And what's happened to Wanna?'

'If he's got any sense, he's curled up somewhere warm.' Jamie stepped onto a flat

rock and looked around in bewilderment.
The rock he was standing on was like a
balcony hanging over the mountainside.
Beneath the balcony, the frozen ground
sloped gently down to a wide valley,
surrounded on both sides by mountains,
covered in a patchy carpet of snow and ice
that stretched as far as Jamie could see.

 26

'There's something strange about this mountainside.' Tom joined Jamie and surveyed the narrow icy ridges and shallow craters in the blue-tinged ground. 'It's creaking and groaning as if it's alive. It reminds me of something . . .'

Just then, Tom lost his footing and skidded into Jamie. Jamie's feet shot out

from under him and the two of them
slipped feet first over the edge of the
ice balcony.

Ooof!

They landed on their bottoms and
began to slide down, down, down.

'I've got it!' Tom yelled. 'The mountain
isn't alive . . . it's moving. We're on a
glacier!'

'Like the one in the movie in Dad's
museum.' Jamie laughed. 'Awesome!'

'Wheeee!' they yelled, whizzing and
bumping down the ice.

The bottom of the glacier was coming
up fast.

'We need to stop,' Jamie said, as they
bumped across a patch of icy ridges. 'How
do we put on the brakes?' He could see
something standing in their path, but he
was juddering about too much to work out
what it was. He dug his heels and elbows

 29

into the glacier, but instead of coming slowly to a halt, it made him spin round and round.

Scrunch!

Jamie landed head-first on the freezing cold gravel at the base of the glacier with Tom spreadeagled next to him.

A reptilian head loomed over them. A very bony head. It tilted to one side, and two beady eyes stared unblinkingly at them. The little dinosaur opened its mouth.

Grunk!

Grunk, grunk!

Grunk!

'Wanna!' Jamie shouted. 'He must have slid down from the cave, like us.'

Their little dinosaur friend bobbed his head up and down and wagged his tail as the boys picked themselves up and brushed themselves down.

Grunk?

Wanna looked hopefully at them.

'He's expecting his favourite snack,' Tom said. 'Stinky gingko fruit.'

'I haven't seen any gingko trees,' Jamie said.

'Maybe there are some around here,' Tom peered through his binoculars. 'No, no gingkoes for Wanna for Christmas.' He sighed. 'All I can see are a few scrubby little plants and some big, dark boulders. That's strange. The boulders are moving . . . '

Tom fiddled with the focus. 'Wow!' Tom shouted, and handed the binoculars to Jamie. 'You're never going to believe this!'

Jamie looked through the binoculars to see that the boulders looked like hairy elephants, with high domed heads and

enormous tusks. 'Woolly mammoths!' he exclaimed, almost dropping the binoculars in surprise. 'You know what that means?'

Tom grinned at Jamie.

'We're in the Ice Age!' they cheered, leaping in the air and giving each other a high five. Wanna leapt up and tried to join in, too.

'But how did we get to the Ice Age?' Jamie asked.

'It's got to be a different fossil,' Tom said.

Jamie nodded. They knew that taking different fossil ammonites with them through their secret cave changed what time period they visited in Dino World. But they only had ammonites from the late Cretaceous and the Jurassic. They didn't have an Ice Age fossil.

Jamie looked through his backpack, but he couldn't find any fossil. 'I must have forgotten to put the Jurassic fossil in my backpack. So *you* must have the fossil.'

 33

'I don't have anything . . . ' Tom patted his pockets. 'Only the present your grandad gave me.'

'That's got to be it,' Jamie said. 'Open it!'

Tom looked unsure. 'But it isn't Christmas yet.'

'I think this is a special circumstance,' Jamie replied.

Jamie and Wanna crowded round Tom as he took off his gloves and peeled the silver tape away. Underneath was a stone that looked like the underside of a shoe. In the icy sunshine, deep wavy lines stood out along the top surface.

Tom grinned from ear to ear. 'It's a tooth!' he said. 'A woolly mammoth tooth. It's so small; it must be from a baby one.'

'Awesome!' Jamie said as Tom stuffed the tooth and the wrapping in his pocket and put his gloves back on. 'We brought an Ice Age fossil with us, so we came out in the Ice Age.'

'And Wanna is part of the magic, so he's come, too,' Jamie said.

A low rumbling noise made them look up. The mammoths were coming closer.

Wanna grunked nervously.

'Mammoths aren't meat-eaters, Wanna.' Tom laughed.

Wanna watched warily as the mammoths stomped towards them, swinging their trunks from side to side. Jamie counted

seven adults in the herd, and a youngster as big as a horse. The adults were taller than elephants, but their ears were much smaller.

The mammoths didn't seem to notice Wanna and the boys. They stopped at a patch of snow and swept their tusks across it, clearing the ice to pluck trunkfuls of the long yellow grass that lay underneath. The little herd was so close that Jamie could hear the grinding of mammoth teeth and the gurgling and grumbling of mammoth stomachs.

Grunk!

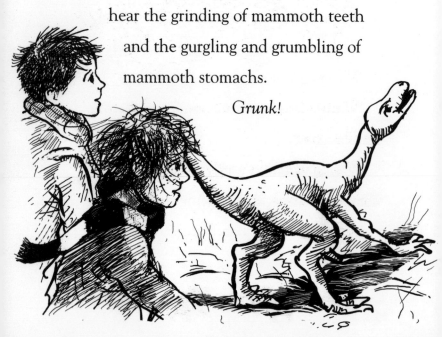

Wanna began to bob his bony head
up and down.

The mammoths stopped eating and
looked up, right at them.

Grunk, grunk!

Wanna stamped his feet.

The mammoths looked at each other.

'They've never seen a
dinosaur before,' Jamie said.

The adult mammoths turned
and lumbered off. Only the
young mammoth stood
its ground and raised
its trunk.

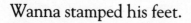

Haroomph!

It gave a loud trumpet.

'Wanna's not that scary,'

Tom said, with a frown.

Grunk,
        grunk,
                grunk!

Wanna head-barged Tom and Jamie
towards the mammoth.

'Hey!' Jamie began, but his words were
drowned by a sound like thunder. He
whirled round. Ice was tumbling down
the glacier and a section of the glacier
as tall and wide as a skyscraper was
breaking away from the
mountainside.

Cra-a-a-ck!

In an instant, Jamie,
Tom, and Wanna were
swept along on the
crest of a glacial
wave.

CHAPTER 3

The wave of ice carried the three friends
across the valley and then rolled to a halt.
Everything went deathly quiet.

Jamie wiped the snow out of his eyes.
All around him had turned into a jumble of
ice. He struggled to his feet, dislodging the
snow that was wedged between his back
and his backpack.

'Tom?' His voice echoed across the icy
landscape.

'I'm here!' What looked like a large snowball shook itself. 'Where's Wanna?'

The boys scanned the white surface.

'There he is!' they said together.

Wanna's head poked out of the snow.

Grunk?

The little dinosaur looked so silly they couldn't help laughing.

'It's only snow, you wombat,' Jamie called. 'Climb out!'

Wanna hauled himself out of the snow.

'He's slower than a snail.' Jamie frowned. 'What's wrong with him?'

'Maybe it's because he's cold blooded,' Tom said. 'His body has chilled, so he can't move fast. He needs to warm up. Help me get him over to that rock.'

Jamie helped push Wanna onto a flat-topped rock where he could bask in the wintry sunshine. Soon, the little wannanosaurus was wagging his tail.

'This will help keep him warm,' Tom said, taking off his warm woolly scarf. He tied it round Wanna's neck.

Jamie laughed. 'Now Wanna's ready to be the first dinosaur to explore the Ice Age,' he said.

Tchooooo!

A sound like a sneeze came from behind them. What looked like a thick hairy stick was poking out of a hill of snow. The stick, as thick as Jamie's leg, bent and waved. It was the trunk of the young woolly mammoth.

The boys and Wanna scrambled towards it. Close up, it looked like a fat, rubbery hair-covered hosepipe.

Harooomph!

The mammoth trumpeted.

Jamie leapt out of the way as the icy mound began to shake and tumble. The young mammoth was lying on its side in a shallow crater in the ice, its powerful legs

 44

scrabbling wildly
against the ice
that kept falling
back on top of it.

Wanna took one look at
the struggling mammoth,
then turned and shot off.

'What's he up to?'
Jamie asked as Wanna
scrabbled and scratched
at a patch of snow. He grabbed
something and scampered back to them.

Wanna deposited a spitty mouthful of
long yellow grass in the snow next to them
and wagged his tail.

'Good idea, Wanna.' Tom held out some
grass towards the frightened mammoth.
The mammoth seemed to smell it and then

45

explored it with the rubbery tip of its shaggy trunk. Then it carefully curled the broad bottom lobe of its trunk around it and put it into its mouth. As the mammoth munched, Jamie crept closer. The young mammoth's curved tusks were as long as brooms with sharp tips.

'It's calmer now,' Tom said. 'Let's try and coax it out with more food.'

'Good idea,' Jamie agreed. He headed to the spot that Wanna had found, kicked more snow off the grass, and returned with a soggy yellow armful. He handed half of the grass to Tom. They crouched beside the shallow crater and held it out to the mammoth.

The mammoth's little ears twitched as it stared at the boys, then, very slowly, it stretched out its trunk and took the grass from Tom.

After a few munches, the mammoth struggled to its feet, sniffing for more. A shower of ice and snow rained from its bushy coat as it chewed.

Jamie backed away, holding his handful of grass high above his head. The young mammoth stepped out of the crater and took the grass. It towered above Jamie like a shaggy mountain. The mammoth seemed to be fine.

'It will go and find its herd now,' Tom said with a smile as they watched the great beast take a few steps away, chewing the grass they had given it.

All around there were tyre-sized mammoth footprints in the snow from when the herd had stampeded away from the avalanche.

 48

Haroomph!

The young mammoth
stopped to examine a
footprint with its trunk. It
turned its head to scan the
lonely landscape. Then its
little ears drooped, and it
slowly swung its trunk, as if it
was unsure which way to go.

'I don't think it knows
how to track its herd,'
Jamie said.

The young mammoth
looked back at them.

Hmph!

It snorted sadly.

Hmph, hmph,
hmph!

Then, suddenly, the mammoth turned
and thundered towards them, stretching out
its trunk. The icy ground shook.

'It'll flatten us!'
Tom yelled as he,
Jamie, and Wanna
fell over each
other in their
hurry to move
out of the
way.

The mammoth
skidded to a halt.
It gently reached
down and felt each of
them with the tip of
its trunk.

'It's OK; it likes us!' Jamie breathed a sigh of relief as warm mammoth breath wafted down his neck. He took off his gloves and gently scratched the mammoth's trunk. 'It's soft under here,' he murmured. 'It's warm and woolly.'

'Woolly!' Tom grinned as they untangled themselves and got to their feet. 'If we follow the mammoth tracks, we can help our new friend Woolly get back to his herd in time for Christmas.'

They set off into the icy valley, following a
confused path of footprints, Tom and Jamie
on either side of Woolly, with Wanna
bounding ahead.

'This must be what your dad called
tundra,' Tom said, as they stomped across
the frozen landscape.

'I'll look it up.' Jamie took out the
Fossil Finder. The Happy Hunting screen
popped up and he typed in '*TUNDRA*'.

'*A VAST TREELESS REGION WITH UNDERLYING FROZEN SOIL CALLED PERMAFROST,*' he read aloud as they plodded along. '*FOUND ONLY IN THE ARCTIC CIRCLE TODAY, BUT COMMON IN THE ICE AGE WHEN IT WAS HOME TO CREATURES LIKE THE WOOLLY MAMMOTH AND THE SABRE-TOOTHED TIGER.*'

'Look!' Tom pointed to a giant pair of curved tusks sticking out from a bank of ice. 'How did a mammoth lose humongous tusks like that?'

Jamie stowed the Fossil Finder in his backpack and went over to take a closer look. 'It's a skeleton!' he said. 'There are lots of bones buried in the ice. Something must have eaten it.'

'A sabre-toothed tiger, maybe,' Tom suggested.

 54

'There'd have been enough meat for a family of sabre-toothed tigers,' Jamie said.

'A whole pride of sabre-toothed tigers,' Tom added.

'All the sabre-toothed tigers in the Ice Age!' Jamie laughed.

Gak, gak, gak.

Wanna shook his head up and down. Then he froze, sniffing the air. Jamie stopped laughing. The little dinosaur was quivering from snout to tail.

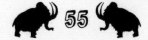

Suddenly there was a strange, high-pitched noise.

'What was that?' Jamie whirled round.

'What?' Tom asked.

'I heard something behind us,' Jamie whispered.

His heart was in his mouth as he and Tom cautiously tiptoed round Woolly's tail end.

'There's nothing there,' Tom murmured, but as he spoke, the sound of eerie laughter echoed across the tundra.

'Someone's following us.' Jamie looked back at the tracks they had left in the snow. A few strides behind them, their prints were overlain by what looked like the footprints of a large dog or cat.

'Not someone. Something.' Tom bent down and examined the footprints. 'Something with sharp claws,' he murmured. 'A meat-eater! It's not following us—it's hunting us!'

'Over there!' The hairs on the back of Jamie's neck prickled as he caught a glimpse of an animal the size of a lion. Its golden tail disappeared behind a boulder a stone's throw away from were they were standing.

Tom and Jamie stared at the boulder. A wolfish snout poked out from behind the rock and opened its powerful fang-lined jaws. The sound of eerie laughter drifted across the tundra again.

'It's a giant hyena!' Tom whispered. 'Their teeth can crunch through bones like butter.'

The hyena emerged from behind the rock. It hunched its lion-like shoulders as it lowered its head and stared at them, ears pricked and alert.

Jamie's stomach did a somersault. They had nothing to defend themselves with, not even a stick. 'Do hyenas hunt in packs?' he asked.

'Sometimes,' Tom said grimly.

A second howl of hysterical laughter joined the first.

'It's a pair!' Tom yelled as the two hyenas charged across the tundra towards them.

For a moment, Wanna, Woolly, Jamie, and Tom were frozen with fear.

'We've got to defend ourselves,' Jamie yelled.

'Yeah, but with what?' Tom asked as they huddled closer to Woolly.

'Throw something at them!' Jamie screamed.

'There's nothing to throw.' Tom looked around wildly. 'Only snow!'

'That's it!' Jamie yelled.

'Snowballs!'

Quickly he scooped up a handful of snow and squashed it in his gloves. He took careful aim.

'Bull's-eye!' he cheered, as he hit the leading hyena on the muzzle.

The hyena shook off the snow and backed away, laughing its horrible laugh. Then it edged forward again. The second hyena snapped at the snowball that whizzed past its ear.

Tom and Jamie hurled volley after volley of hard, icy snowballs. The hyenas weaved and dodged through the snowball blizzard,

snapping and snarling ferociously when one hit home.

'It's no good!' Tom groaned. The hyenas were getting closer and closer, foaming at the jaws.

'We're just making them mad,' Jamie agreed.

Woolly lifted his trunk and trumpeted in fear. The lead hyena flattened its ears and wrinkled its muzzle.

'It's about to spring!' Tom gasped.

With a ferocious snarl, the hyena hurled itself at Woolly's neck.

CHAPTER 5

SEARCH:

In a flash, Wanna jumped out in front of
the hyena. In mid-air, the little dinosaur
collided with the lead hyena, head on.

Thump!

Wanna and the hyena landed heavily
on the ground. The hyena froze.

'It's the first time it's met a dinosaur,'
Tom gasped.

Wanna lowered his bony head and
kicked his feet.

'He's revving up,' Jamie said.

'Go, Wanna, go!' the boys shouted,
as the little dinosaur hurtled towards
the hyena.

Thunk!

Wanna head-butted the hyena, sending
it reeling into its companion.

The hyenas struggled groggily to their
feet and looked at each other.

Wanna lowered his
head once more and kicked
his feet.

Aeeeeeee!

The hyenas tucked their tails between their legs and ran off into the distance as fast as their legs would carry them.

'Wanna saved us!' Jamie cheered.

Wanna wagged his tail happily as the boys tackled him in a great big hug.

Woolly stood apart, slowly swinging his trunk from side to side.

'It's OK, Woolly; the hyenas have gone,' Jamie said, patting the young mammoth's trunk.

Woolly pushed his trunk into one of the mammoth footprints ahead of him. His hairy shoulders sagged and his ears drooped.

'He's missing his family,' Tom said. 'Let's get moving and find the herd.'

The
mammoths'
tracks led them
through a gap in the icy
mountains, out into a
narrow river valley.
Jamie looked at the
rushing torrent of water
that blocked their way.
Small icebergs bobbed and
swirled down it.

'The mammoth herd
must have crossed the river,'

he said. 'I can see their footprints on the other side.'

'Maybe we can jump from ice block to ice block, like moving stepping stones?' Tom suggested.

'But if we slip, we won't last a minute in that icy water,' Jamie told him. 'We'll freeze to death. We should make a raft.' He looked round for some wood, but there was nothing growing but lichens, grasses, and mosses, and a few stunted shrubs.

'If other mammoths have crossed it, so can Woolly,' Tom said. 'He doesn't feel

the cold like we do. He'll just have to find his herd on his own.' Tom picked a handful of grass and waved it in front of Woolly's trunk, then held it out above the river.

Woolly stretched out his trunk and grabbed the grass, but refused to budge.

'We'd better give him a push,' Jamie sighed.

'It's for his own good.'

Jamie, Tom, and Wanna leant against Woolly's hairy behind and together they tried to shove Woolly into the water. Woolly raised his trunk and trumpeted. *Haroomph!*

He turned and lumbered up river, along the bank.

'No, Woolly!' Tom said. 'You're supposed to *cross* the river.'

Jamie, Tom, and Wanna hurried after him. Woolly had stopped by a rocky outcrop that jutted over the river. Here, the river was wider and slower. The bank of the river was dented with icy mammoth footprint-sized puddles.

'Clever Woolly! He's found where the other mammoths crossed,' Tom said, as they watched the young mammoth wade a couple of steps into the river.

Woolly suddenly stopped and turned his head back to the bank. He looked at Jamie, Tom, and Wanna, then swung his trunk out over the water.

'He wants us to cross the river with him,' Jamie said.

'But Woolly's got fur to keep him warm,' Tom replied. 'We haven't.'

Oooomph!

Woolly trumpeted softly.

'There's only one thing for it,' Tom said. 'If Woolly wants us to go with him, he'll have to take us on his back.'

'Awesome idea!' Jamie scrambled up the pile of slippery rocks that jutted out over the river. He leaned across to Woolly and grabbed a handful of the mammoth's hair.

'There's plenty to hang on to,' he said, hoisting himself onto Woolly's broad back.

Woolly stopped swinging his trunk and made pleased oomphing noises as Tom scrambled up behind Jamie.

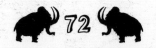 72

'Come on, Wanna!' they called. The little dinosaur tilted his head to one side, then launched himself at the icy rocks, scrabbling wildly with all four feet. At the top of the rocks, he hurled himself onto Woolly's back. Jamie and Tom had to grab hold of him to stop him hurtling off the other side.

'Hold on tight!' Jamie yelled as Woolly lurched into the river.

They clung on to Woolly's hairy back as he waded across. Ice blocks floated past them.

'This river is getting deeper,' Jamie said, as the water rose up past Woolly's knees. Woolly raised his trunk. 'Elephants do that when they go swimming. It's like a snorkel,' he added nervously.

'It's Woolly's swimming trunk,' Tom joked.

Jamie chuckled, but was also starting to worry at how deep the river was becoming. The icy water was lapping around Woolly's middle. Tom, Jamie, and Wanna drew up their feet.

'The other mammoths got across,' Tom repeated, but he didn't sound so sure.

'But the other mammoths were bigger than Woolly.' Jamie held his breath as the little mammoth began to swim.

 74

The current started to sweep them down
the ice-cold river.

'Woolly's out of his depth,' Jamie yelled.
'And that means we are, too!'

CHAPTER 6

SEARCH:

For a few terrifying seconds, they bobbed
and swirled down the river like an iceberg,
but Woolly was a strong swimmer, and soon
Jamie felt the young mammoth's feet
scrabble on the river bed.

'Woolly knew what he was doing when he
picked that spot,' Tom said, as the mammoth
took them ashore right opposite the place
where they had originally wanted to cross.

77

'It's like it was instinctive,' Jamie agreed as they clambered down from Woolly's back. 'Mammoths must have been crossing here for hundreds of years.'

'Thousands of years,' Tom said.

'Millions of years,' Jamie said automatically. 'Hang on—mammoths weren't around that long,' he corrected himself.

Woolly stretched out his trunk and tail.

'Stand back,' warned Tom and dived out of the way. Woolly shook himself from the tip of his hairy trunk to the end of his tufty tail and freezing cold water droplets splattered all over Jamie.

Brrr! Jamie shivered.

'We'd better keep moving, before you turn into an Ice Age ice man!' Tom grinned.

78

They left the river behind them and
followed the mammoth tracks between the
snow-covered mountains on either side.
Here, where the sunshine was trapped
between the mountains, there was less ice
and snow.

The ground was a patchwork of deep red
lichens, bright emerald mosses, and tufts of
yellowy grass. Here and there, scrubby bushes

with woody stems and small grey-green leaves
grew between the rocks. A chilly breeze was
blowing down the valley and Jamie's and
Woolly's coats steamed as they dried.

Wanna sniffed suspiciously at a patch
of lichens.

'He's hungry,' Tom said.

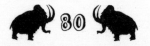

'Everything's different from what he's used to.' Jamie frowned. 'The tundra's too cold for gingko trees to grow.'

'There are some cones on this bush. Perhaps he'll eat these.' Tom pulled a handful of small cones off a low bush and held them out for Wanna.

The little dinosaur
sniffed at them,
then stuck out his
sandpaper tongue and
licked one suspiciously.

Grunk!

His tail wagged and he gobbled
up the cones. Long strings of dino drool
dribbled from his mouth. He looked round
hopefully, and spotted a thicket of cone-
bearing shrubs ahead.

'He's happy now,' Tom said, as they
watched Wanna dart off.

Wanna disappeared into the waist-high
thicket. They could hear him grunking
contentedly every time he found a cluster
of tasty cones.

Grunk, grunk.

Then, a strange, strangled cry came out of the shrubs.

Woolly stopped in his tracks.

'That didn't sound like Wanna,' Tom said.

Aaaaaah!

A shiver ran down Jamie's spine. 'That sounded like a scream,' he whispered.

'It's probably a bird screeching,' Tom said. 'Or maybe a fox.'

There was a rustling noise and a loud *grunk!* Wanna shot out of the shrubs and dashed to them. He stood in front of the boys, repeatedly turning his head towards the bush.

The boys held their breath and listened.

Uuuh.

Uuuh.

It was a different noise, but it came from the same place as before.

'That didn't sound like a fox or a bird,' Jamie murmured.

Wanna skirted round behind them and lowered his bony skull. Gently but firmly, he nudged first Jamie, then Tom, towards the low shrubs.

The boys looked at each other.

'He wants us to go in there,' Tom said.

Uuuuuh! The noise came again.

'It doesn't sound very fierce,' Jamie said. 'We should check it out.'

He crawled into the thicket, closely followed by Tom and Wanna.

Between the shrubs ahead of them, something furry was sitting on the ground.

84

'It could be a little bear,' Tom whispered, as they edged closer. 'A bear with a stick!' He pointed to a long thin pole lying on the ground next to the creature.

Uuuh! The creature lifted its head. It was dressed from head to toe in what looked like a patchwork of leather and furs, and it had clear, blue eyes looking at them from a dirty, hairless face.

'It's not a bear,' Jamie gasped. 'It's a boy, like us!'

At the sound of Jamie's voice, the boy grabbed his stick. It was tipped with sharpened antler. Jamie's heart skipped a beat. It was just like the spear in his dad's museum.

'*Yaaar!*' the boy yelled, thrusting his spear towards them.

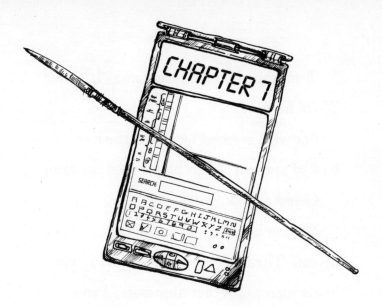

CHAPTER 7

SEARCH:

Jamie and Tom backed into Wanna. They
stared at the boy in amazement. They'd
never come across another human being
in any of their adventures before.

Yaaarr! The boy pushed his dark,
straggly hair out of his eyes, and waved his
spear at them again.

'Hello,' Jamie called softly, sitting back
on his heels and holding up his empty
hands.

Tom smiled and did the same. 'It's OK. We're friends.'

For what seemed like ages, the boy looked at them. Then he lowered his spear.

Grunk, grunk, grunk.

Wanna bounced up to the boy, wagging his tail. The boy's eyes widened with fear. 'Early man never met dinosaurs,' Jamie whispered to Tom.

The boy grabbed his spear and tried to kick himself backwards, away from Wanna, but winced in pain.

'There's something wrong with his ankle,' Tom said.

The boy waved his spear threateningly at Wanna. Wanna lunged forward and grabbed it in his scaly jaws.

'*Aaaah!*'
screamed the boy.

'It's OK. Wanna's
a friend, too.'

Jamie took the
spear off Wanna. It was
made of a sharpened antler
point bound onto the split
end of a long stick with narrow
strips of hide. Jamie handed
it back to the terrified boy.

The boy looked amazed. Then he smiled
nervously at them. Wanna lay down next
to the boy, and nudged him gently, making
little grunking noises.

'I'm Jamie,' said Jamie, pointing to his
chest. 'This is Tom, and Wanna.' He pointed
to each in turn.

'Amie, Om, Wanna,' the boy repeated. He smiled and pointed to his own chest. '*Eguntsenti-itzotz*,' he said.

Tom and Jamie looked at each other in surprise. The boy's long name sounded like a series of clicks and grunts.

'Egg what?' Jamie spluttered

'Eg gunt sent tea itz otz,' the boy repeated slowly. Jamie and Tom tried hard to copy him. The boy laughed and held up his hand.

'Egg,' he said.

'Egg,' Tom and Jamie repeated.

'What happened to your ankle, Egg?' Jamie pointed to the boy's leg and raised his eyebrows.

Egg started to tell them in his own language, then, seeing they didn't

Egg what?

understand, he used two fingers on one hand to show that he was walking on the mountain. Then he swept his hands to his side in a rush, and showed something falling down the mountain into his path.

'I think he's telling us he was up on the mountain, and he was in an avalanche,' Tom said, nodding encouragingly.

Egg made movements with his hands as if he was running away, then showed him falling.

91

'He must have fallen badly,' Jamie said.

Still telling his story, Egg looked from side to side. Then he shook his head sadly.

'I get it,' Tom said. 'He was looking for someone—his family maybe—but he couldn't find them.'

Jamie looked at Egg and nodded. 'Can we take a look at your ankle, Egg?'

The boy seemed to understand. He grimaced with pain and pulled the bottom of his thick leather trousers out of his fur boot.

'No blood,' Jamie murmured. 'That's good. It's swollen and sore-looking, but there are no bones sticking out. I think it's just a sprain.' He smiled at Egg as the boy painfully pulled his boot back on.

'He's in trouble if he can't get to shelter

by nightfall,' Tom said. 'The hyenas or the sabre-toothed tigers will get him. We have to help him get back to his family.'

'But we haven't seen any sign of other human beings,' Jamie said with a frown. 'Where does your family live, Egg?' Jamie pointed at Egg, then put his arms around Tom and Wanna's shoulders to try and show what he meant.

Egg just looked confused.

Behind them, there was a crashing in the undergrowth.

'Woolly!'
Tom laughed as
the little mammoth
curled his trunk gently around his neck
in greeting.

'Mamut!' Egg's eyes opened wide.
He babbled excitedly as he pulled out a
hide thong from around his neck.
Something dangled from it. He held it
out for Jamie and Tom to see. It was a

small ivory carving of a mammoth.

'Mamut,' he repeated, pointing to Woolly.

'Mamut,' Jamie and Tom said.

They all grinned.

'Mammoth must be really important to Egg's people,' Tom told Jamie. 'Your dad said they followed the herds . . .'

'So if we take Egg with us, we should find his family when we find Woolly's herd,' Jamie said. 'Now we have two Christmas presents to deliver—one boy and one mammoth.'

Jamie and Tom helped Egg to stand on his good foot, and together they half-carried him out of the thicket. He leant his weight on his spear, but as soon as he tried to take a step on his bad ankle, he collapsed with a cry of pain.

'We can get him up on Woolly's back,' Jamie said, manoeuvring the young mammoth up beside a low rock.

'Get up on the mammoth, Egg,' Tom

pointed to Egg then to the rock
and then to Woolly's back.

'Up?' Egg looked confused for
a moment, then he grinned.

Jamie held Egg's spear with one
hand and steadied Woolly with the
other as Tom helped Egg up on to
the rock, then boosted him up so
he could haul himself onto Woolly's
hairy back. Jamie handed Egg his
spear. Egg laid his spear across his
lap and clapped his hands.

'Egg. Up. Mamut!' he yelled
in glee.

'I don't think Egg's ever ridden
on a mammoth before,' Jamie said.

'Welcome to Egg's Ice Age
adventure!' Tom said in his

best announcer voice as they walked along beside Woolly. 'This is Tom Clay reporting for Tundra TV. Here we are, with our friend Egg, the Early Modern Man, tracking the footprints of woolly mammoths across a wintry, wild, and windy landscape. What else will we discover on our cool Christmas adven—?'

'Reindeer!' Jamie interrupted him. 'Over there, a whole herd!'

'Awesome!' Tom exclaimed, forgetting his commentary. 'Reindeer at Christmas. Is there one with a red nose?'

Jamie pointed to a reindeer that was chewing on a mouthful of red lichen. 'That one.' Its nose was plastered with lichen juice.

'And there's something else behind Rudolph.' Tom pulled out his binoculars. 'A woolly rhino!'

Jamie took the binoculars and watched the two-horned hairy rhino trundle past the

herd of reindeer and off along the foot of the mountains. Jamie was so busy watching the rhino he didn't look where he was going. His foot crunched into something. It was a huge pat of mammoth dung. It sank through the crust into the pooey goo beneath.

Yeuch! Jamie tried to scrape off the stinky dung.

'It's fresh, not frozen.' Tom laughed. 'That means the mammoth herd can't be far away.'

They trekked on. The valley was narrowing, and mountains to either side of them rose up like cliffs, funnelling them alongside the icy stream. The tundra landscape was changing, too. A few small willow trees had found enough soil to put down roots, and the grass grew greener, interspersed with tiny plants dotted with purple flowers. Woolly grabbed a trunkful and chewed them slowly as they went along. Ahead, the mammoth tracks disappeared around a bend in the valley.

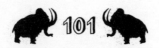

Up on Woolly's back, Egg pointed towards the bank of the stream, making clicking and grunting noises.

Jamie and Tom glanced over at what looked like more piles of dung. As they watched, one of the bear-sized dung piles moved. It had a broad, paddle-like tail.

'That's a giant beaver,' Tom said in amazement.

'A whole family of giant beavers,' Jamie added as, one by one, the beavers plopped into the stream and swam off.

'It's amazing they find enough to eat,' Tom said.

'Eat,' Egg repeated.

'No, the beavers aren't called eat,' Jamie pointed into his mouth and rubbed his tummy. 'Eat,' he repeated.

'Eat.' Egg pointed to the plants Woolly had been eating, then pointed into *his* mouth and rubbed *his* tummy.

'We can eat these?' Tom bent down and pulled up a handful.

Wanna looked on curiously as
Jamie did the same.

The plants had a stringy stem and
tiny spiky leaves ending in curly tendrils.
Tom brushed off the cold soil from the fat
tube-like roots and handed them up to Egg.
He munched up every bit.

Jamie tried a nibble and pulled a face.
'It tastes like a mixture of sprouts and

Gak!

stale peas,' he said, giving
the rest to Wanna. The
little dinosaur immediately
spat them out.

Gak!

Tom and Jamie fell around laughing.
'Amie, Om, Wanna!' Egg pointed up at
the sky. Dark clouds were rolling
across it. An icy wind gusted up the

valley and tiny white snowflakes began to swirl around them.

'Snow!' Jamie said delightedly, watching Wanna snap at a passing flake.

'It's a white Christmas after all,' Tom said.

Wanna didn't seem so impressed.

Gak, gak, gak!

Egg was looking up at the sky with a worried look. He babbled something. Seeing that Tom and Jamie didn't understand, he put his hands over his eyes.

'Egg's trying to warn us,' Jamie said. 'Maybe we need to find shelter.'

In an instant, it was snowing heavily. The tops of the mountains disappeared from view. Wanna's head drooped. He looked cold and miserable.

'Amie, Om, Wanna!'
Egg pointed to the cliffs. A
path led up into the rocks.

'Maybe Egg thinks
there's shelter up there.'
Jamie grabbed Woolly's
trunk and pulled him
towards it.

Another icy blast
ripped through the valley
and they were blinded by a
swirling tornado of snow.

'It's a blizzard!' Tom
shouted, grabbing Jamie's
sleeve. 'Keep hold of
each other!'

Haroomph!

Woolly trumpeted wildly.

'Woolly's freaking out!' Jamie yelled.
'He must be remembering the avalanche!'

'He'll trample us if he's not careful,'
Tom groaned.

Woolly began stamping his feet and
shaking his tusks. He stepped to one side,
knocking over Wanna, and then backed up
towards Jamie and Tom, who dived out of
the way towards a slightly dazed Wanna.
At least Egg was safe up on his back.

But then, through the swirling snow,
Jamie saw Woolly's hairy leg rise up high
into the air, about to come crashing down
on top of him!

Just in time, Jamie rolled away as Woolly's foot came down, covering him in a snow shower.

Jamie shook the snow out of his face, but now all he could see was hair. He, Tom, and Wanna were wrapped in a hairy blanket!

'Amie, Om, Wanna,' Egg's voice came from somewhere above.

Jamie caught his breath. The three of them were half buried in a pile of snow,

with the young mammoth standing
over them.

'We've got to get everyone somewhere
safe,' Jamie said, looking at Wanna
shivering, despite the warmth from Woolly.

Tom and Jamie pushed the
reluctant little dinosaur out into the
snow, and Tom stroked Woolly's
trunk. 'Calm down and we'll
get you away from the
storm,' Tom said.

Woolly seemed
to listen, and Egg
urged him on.

Jamie, Tom, and Wanna followed closely
behind the young mammoth as he cleared
a path through the snow with his tusks.
Jamie's skin stung as snow blew into
his face. His eyelashes were so full
of snowflakes it was impossible to
see where they were going.
Then, all of a
sudden, the snow
stopped.

Jamie caught his breath as he shook the snow out of his eyes and looked up. They were beneath a rocky overhang. Outside, the snow was still falling hard and fast all around.

'I'm so glad we found Egg,' Tom said as Egg scrambled down from Woolly's back. 'We never would have found shelter on our own.'

Egg leant on his spear and Tom and
Jamie helped him hobble beneath the
overhang. It opened into a wide shallow cave.
It was too low for Woolly, but he was safe and
out of the snow under the rock ledge.

Jamie pulled out his torch and flicked it
on to see into the cave.

'Ugh!' Egg grunted, and stared at the
electronic device. He waved his hand in
front of the beam of light cautiously, as if it
might burn him. Then he grinned and
reached out for the torch.

Jamie handed it to him.

'He can't have seen anything like it.'
Tom laughed as Egg examined the torch
and then shone it right into his own eyes.

'Uuurgh!' he exclaimed, dropping the torch.

It clattered on the stone floor and went out.

As Egg stumbled around, temporarily blinded, Jamie picked up the torch. 'The bulb's broken,' he groaned.

'Never mind,' Tom said. 'There's just enough light to see.'

They peered through the gloom. Half-burnt logs were scattered around the rocky floor.

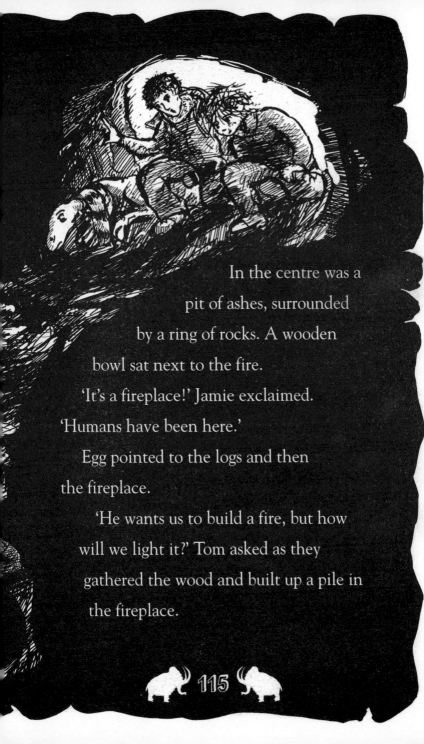

In the centre was a
pit of ashes, surrounded
by a ring of rocks. A wooden
bowl sat next to the fire.

'It's a fireplace!' Jamie exclaimed.
'Humans have been here.'

Egg pointed to the logs and then
the fireplace.

'He wants us to build a fire, but how
will we light it?' Tom asked as they
gathered the wood and built up a pile in
the fireplace.

'I'm not sure,' Jamie replied.

Gruuuunk!

Wanna dragged over a log, too.

When they were done, Egg hobbled to the back of the cave. The boys helped him over to it and watched in semi-darkness as he picked up a handful of shadowy things from a rocky ledge before hobbling back to the fireplace.

'Dried straw,' Tom said, as Egg laid a handful in the centre of the logs. 'That catches fire easily.'

Egg held something out for them to see. It was a rough nodule of flint that fitted comfortably into his hand. With a grunt of pain, Egg knelt beside the old hearth and pulled out a leather pouch on a long leather thong from around his neck. He took out a golf ball-sized lump of shiny black rock.

Jamie and Tom watched spellbound as
Egg struck the stone with the flint.

Sparks leapt into the straw and set it alight.

'Awesome!' Jamie and Tom said together.
Egg smiled as he stowed his firestone back
into his pouch.

The straw lit the dry tinder and soon the
fire was burning brightly, lighting up
more of the cave. At the back,
on one side, Jamie could
make out narrow strips of
dried leather flapping
from a short pole
that rested
between two
rocky
ledges.

Egg gestured to a piece the length of his arm, then to his ankle.

'A bandage! Good idea.' Jamie retrieved the leather strip and he and Tom helped Egg bind up his ankle.

Egg leant on his spear and did a couple of quick laps round the fire with a big grin on his face.

'That's much better. He can support his weight now,' Tom applauded.

Wanna got up, wagging his tail.

'Wanna's warmed up, too,' Jamie said.

'The fire's burning the wood pretty quickly, though,' Tom said, looking around for more logs.

Egg pointed to what looked like thick brown pancakes at the side of the cave and the boys loaded them into the hearth and

watched the fire burn steadily, with a slightly blue flame.

'Dried mammoth dung burns a treat,' Tom chuckled.

'That's dried mammoth dung? Gross!' Jamie rushed out to the overhang and stuck his hands into a pile of snow that had built up all around it.

Woolly stood watching as he rubbed it into his hands.

'Woolly's fine, but it's still snowing,' Jamie reported. 'We'll have to stay here for a while. Anyone want a sandwich?' He opened the foil pack of Grandad's cheese and pickle sandwiches and held them out to Tom, Wanna, and Egg.

Gak!

Gak!

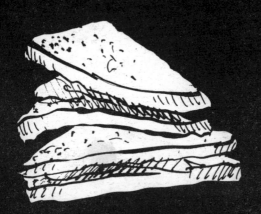

Wanna backed away and Egg sniffed at them suspiciously.

'Yum!' Tom said loudly, taking one and gobbling it down. 'Tastes a bit dungy. Maybe I should have washed my hands, too . . .'

Egg took a big bite. His eyes began to water.

'Whoops! Should've warned him about Grandad's blow-your-brains-out pickle . . .' Jamie mumbled with his mouth full.

Egg put down the remains of his sandwich, grabbed the wooden bowl by the fire and came back with the bowl full of snow. He took a handful of snow to cool down his mouth and set the bowl next to the fire. Then, he grabbed the rest of his sandwich.

'Yum!' he said enthusiastically, gobbling it down. Then he took a long drink of melted snow, and passed it to the boys who each took a sip.

Tom, Jamie, Egg, and Wanna basked in the warmth of the fire, eating their lunch.

Shadows flickered on the cave wall, and Jamie started to get a spooky feeling. They were thousands of years in the past, hiding from a blizzard in a pre-historic cave. What if the person who made this cave came back and wasn't as friendly as Egg? Anything could happen.

Jamie was about to whisper something to Tom when suddenly something grabbed him from behind!

CHAPTER 10

SEARCH:

Jamie leapt up, dropped the last bite of his sandwich, and whirled round to find Tom there with a grin on his face.

'I got you good.' Tom couldn't stop laughing, and Egg chuckled, too.

Even Wanna grunked along.

'Alright, alright,' Jamie said, sitting back down by the fire. He was glad it was just his friend, but there was something about this cave that was spooky.

'This is a perfect place to tell
ghost stories,' Jamie said,

stuffing the empty foil wrapper into his
backpack.

'Great idea,' Tom said.

'But Egg won't be able to
understand anything we say,'
Jamie said. 'Let's do shadow
puppets instead.' He put his
hands together and made the
shape of a bird. The fire
threw the shadow of a huge
bird onto the cave wall.
Jamie waggled his fingers
to make the bird's
wings flap.

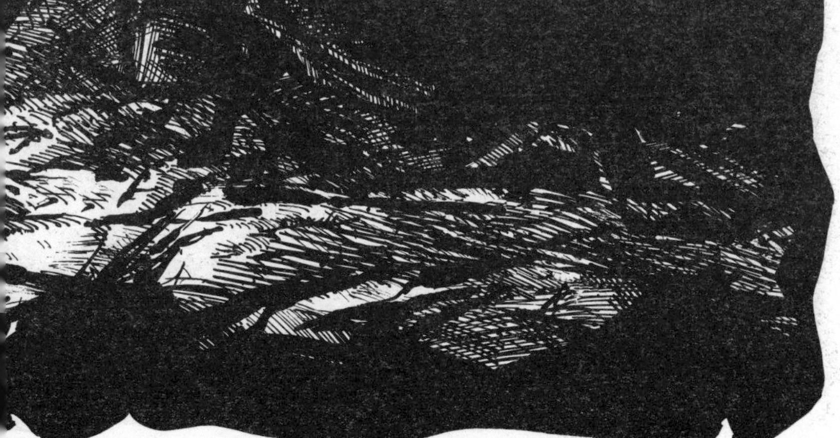

Egg clapped his hands. Then he made a fist with one hand and stuck out three fingers. A life-like mammoth sprang to life on the cave walls. Quickly, Egg positioned his other hand. A man with a spear appeared on the wall.

'Awesome!' Jamie breathed. 'He's an expert.'

'I can make up a story from this.' Tom spoke in a low, dramatic voice. 'Man hunts mammoth with his spear, but mammoth won't be hunted easily. The mammoth charges after the hunter, chasing him to the edge of a cliff. The hunter dodges, just in time. He throws

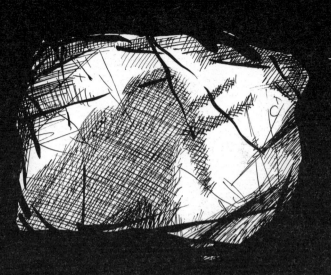

himself to one side. The mammoth tumbles over the cliff . . . '

Egg grinned at Tom and Jamie and then made a different shape with his hand. It was a four-legged animal with a tail and stalked slowly across the wall: a sabre-toothed tiger with huge canines!

'Now the man is being hunted,' Tom whispered, 'by the fiercest predator of the Ice Age!'

'Yaaaarl,' Egg snarled, making the shadow of the big cat leap across the cave walls.

Yaaarrrrl! A snarl echoed round the cave.

Jamie's blood ran cold. He glanced around fearfully, but all he could see were the dancing shadows made by the fire.

Egg grabbed his spear and leapt to his feet.

Grrrrr.

The noise was coming from the passageway at the back of the cave.

Jamie held his breath as a powerful tiger-like beast padded slowly out of the shadows.

'It must have been sheltering in the cave, too,' Tom whispered as the sabre-toothed tiger stalked towards them.

Egg shook his spear at it.

Sppth!

It hissed at them.

'It looks mad,' Jamie said as the sabre-tooth slowly advanced with its ears flattened and its eyes glowing red in the firelight. It snarled, baring its long curved fangs.

Jamie grabbed a smouldering stick from the edge of the fire and waved it at the creature.

Yarrrl.

The sabre-tooth backed away.

'Good idea!' Tom yelled.

He and Egg grabbed burning sticks from the fire and, together with Jamie, they waved them in front of the sabre-tooth, making sure Wanna stayed safely behind them. The tiger's huge shadow prowled across the cave walls as they backed out of the cave towards Woolly. As they retreated, the sabre-tooth slunk after them.

'These sticks won't burn for ever,' Jamie whispered. 'And we can't outrun it. What are we going to do?'

Outside, the blizzard had stopped. They stepped back into a thick layer of snow. Beneath the overhang, Woolly was standing to one side, stamping from foot to foot, swinging his trunk and tusks. As soon as he saw the boy's flaming sticks, he backed away in alarm, right into the cave wall.

Swhoosh!

The boys and Wanna jumped out of the way as a mini avalanche of new snow from the blizzard landed in a heap in front of the cave.

Yaarrl!

The sabre-tooth snarled ferociously, but took a step further back into the cave.

'Keep waving the sticks!' Jamie bellowed, passing his to Tom. He grabbed Woolly by the trunk. If he could get the mammoth to bump the cave wall again, he might bring down enough snow to block the sabre-tooth in.

'The sticks are going out. We can't hold it back much longer!' Tom yelled.

Woolly suddenly caught sight of the spitting, snarling sabre-tooth. The young mammoth's eyes widened in fear. He shook Jamie's hand off his trunk, and backed into the cave wall, trumpeting wildly.

The sabre-tooth crouched, ready to pounce.

'Hurry!' Tom shouted. 'The sabre-tooth's almost on us.'

Woolly barged into the wall once more
and a thick ledge of snow slid down the
overhang. Tom grabbed Egg and pulled
him out of the way.

Whoosh!

The snow came tumbling down in a
thick drift, blocking off the entrance to
the cave.

Woolly trumpeted in triumph, then fell
quiet. They could hear the sabre-tooth on

the other side snarling and
scrabbling at the loosely
packed snow.

'That's not going to keep
it in for long,' Tom said.
He looked at Jamie.

'Run!' they agreed.

Tom, Jamie, Egg, and
Wanna hurled themselves
down the mountain—and
sank up to their knees in
the deep snow. Woolly
plodded behind them.

'Let's get up on
Woolly!' Jamie yelled.
He and Tom
boosted Egg and
Wanna onto

Woolly's back, then they pulled themselves up on the mammoth's shaggy coat. Jamie sat in front, clinging to the back of Woolly's domed head as the young mammoth plunged through the thick snow, down to the valley below.

'There's no sign of the sabre-tooth,' Tom called from Woolly's rear end. 'He must have decided to look for an easier meal.'

At the bottom of the valley, the snow was shallower. They couldn't see the mammoth herd's footprints any more but Tom remembered which way they had been heading. The group made quick progress along the river bank, following the valley as it bent south and began to widen. Here the bushes were greener and laden with juicy blue berries.

Tom pointed to a steaming pile of mammoth dung. 'It's warm. They can't be far away.'

Woolly raised his trunk.

Harooomph!

He broke into a trot, rounded the corner and skidded to a halt at the entrance to a wide green valley. Ahead, a herd of mammoths looked up from the rich grazing ground. They raised their trunks when they saw Woolly.

Haroomph!

They all called out to him.

Jamie, Tom, Egg, and Wanna scrambled down from Woolly's back and stood back as the young mammoth ran to his herd. The other mammoths caressed him gently with their trunks, making happy snorting noises, all the while keeping their eyes on the boys and Wanna.

'They think we're hunters,' Jamie murmured, as the herd of mammoths

plodded off. Woolly turned and raised
his trunk.

'He's saying goodbye.' Tom and Jamie
waved back, Egg raised his spear and
Wanna wagged his tail as the mammoths
disappeared into the distance.

Egg stood scanning the horizon.
Suddenly, he gestured with his spear.
A huge smile spread across his face. Jamie
and Tom followed his gaze. At the edge of

the valley, smoke was circling into the air.

'It's a fire,' Tom said. 'It must be Egg's family.'

Egg pointed to the fire, then in turn to Jamie, Tom, and Wanna.

'He wants us to go with him.' Jamie beamed.

'We can't,' Tom said, crouching down. 'We should keep out of sight. If any more Ice Age people see us with a dinosaur, we could mess up prehistory. As it is, Egg's family will never believe him when he tells them who he was with.'

'They'll think he imagined it all,' Jamie agreed, dropping to his knees. He pulled Wanna down beside him.

'We have to go back now, Egg.' Tom
gestured to himself, Jamie, and Wanna,
then pointed back along the valley.

Egg's face fell, but he seemed to
understand. He raised his spear, then gave
them a dazzling smile and limped away.
They waved after him. After a few steps,
Egg half-turned and waved back.

Tom took out his binoculars.
'There's a hide-covered tent, like
a tepee,' he said, handing the
binoculars to Jamie.

In front of the tepee, Jamie could
make out a group of about ten early
humans huddled around an open
fire. They jumped to their feet

as Egg approached, then rushed forward with open arms. As they hugged, Jamie handed the binoculars back to Tom. Shouts of joy echoed round the valley.

'Job done,' Jamie said, giving Tom a high five. 'Egg and Woolly are both back with their families for Christmas. Now, let's get back to ours in time for the party!'

Tom took one last look through the binoculars. 'They're dancing round the fire,' he laughed. 'They're having a Christmas party, too!'

CHAPTER 12

Sunshine twinkled on the freshly fallen snow as Tom and Jamie led Wanna back towards the glacier. Now that the wind had died down, it didn't seem so cold.

Jamie wondered how they were going to cross the river without Woolly, but there was no need to worry. So much snow had fallen that an arch had formed over the icy water, making a bridge that was solid enough for them to cross.

The three friends picked their way across the ice field where the glacier had fallen, clambered up the glacier itself, and slithered back to the ice cave.

'All that exercise has warmed me up,' Jamie panted.

'Me too,' Tom gasped.

Grunk!

Wanna spotted a low pine cone bush growing beside the cave and began to gobble down the cones.

'It's made Wanna hungry,' Jamie said.

Wanna turned his head to one side.
His beady eyes looked first at Tom,
then at Jamie. Then he bobbed his
head, broke off a short pine cone laden
branch and trotted over to them.

Grunk, he said, dropping it at their feet.

'Wanna's giving us a Christmas present,'
Tom said. 'Thanks, Wanna!'

'I almost forgot.' Jamie rummaged in
his backpack. 'This is for you, Wanna.' He
unwrapped the slab of birdseed cake, broke off
a piece, and handed it to the little dinosaur.

Wanna gobbled it down.

Grunk, grunk, grunk!

He circled round and round in glee,
shaking off the scarf Tom had lent him.

'It's a happy dance!' Tom said, circling
round with his arms out.

Jamie joined in, too.

They fell down in a dizzy heap in the snow, laughing.

'It's time to say goodbye,' Jamie said at last, giving Wanna the rest of the birdseed cake and giving Tom back his scarf.

'Happy Christmas, Wanna!' Tom and Jamie shouted. And, as the little dinosaur joyfully munched up the rest of his present, they stepped backwards into the icy fossil footprints. In an instant, they were back in the velvety darkness of the secret cave in Dinosaur Cove.

Jamie grabbed Tom's sleeve and together they groped along the

cold cave walls until they found the gap
that led into the smugglers' cave. They
dashed out of the cave, and stood,
blinking, in bright sunlight. Dinosaur
Cove was a sparkling Christmassy
winter wonderland.

'Awesome!' Tom gasped. 'It's snowed here, too.'

'It's like the Ice Age,' Jamie said as they skidded down the path towards the beach.

'Ahoy there, me hearties!' Grandad looked up from the giant snowman he was making on the beach. 'Did the wildlife enjoy that Christmas present I gave you?'

Jamie looked at Tom. 'Sure did!' they said together.

'How do you like my snowman?'
Grandad stuck two ammonite fossils on the
head for eyes and a belemnite for the nose.

'Cool!' Jamie gathered a handful of
snow and squished it together to make a
snowball. 'I'll make a snow dinosaur,'
he said, starting to roll the snowball
along the ground,
picking up more
and more snow.

'What about you, Tom?' Grandad asked.

'I'm going to build a snow baby woolly mammoth,' Tom said, picking up a couple of tusk-shaped pieces of driftwood. 'It will have a domed forehead and great long curved tusks.'

'Don't forget the tiny ears and tail . . . ' Jamie said.

' . . . and that lippy bit on the end of his tusk . . . ' Tom added.

'You two know a lot about mammoths.' Grandad's eyes twinkled. 'Anyone would think you'd met one.'

Jamie and Tom grinned at one another.

'We're hoping to meet Father Christmas next!' Tom said.

'Are you, indeed?' Grandad smiled at them. 'Well, you never know what you will find in Dinosaur Cove!'

'That's true,' Jamie laughed, thinking
of Egg and Woolly with their families in
the Ice Age, and Wanna curled up safe
and warm in the Cretaceous. 'Dinosaur
Cove is full of surprises. It's like Christmas
every day!'

ICE AGE WORLD

Ice Cave

Glacier

Valley

----- BOYS' ROUTE

 156

Sabre-
Toothed
Tiger cave

Steppe
Tundra

157

GLOSSARY

Avalanche – a fall of snow down a slope. It can be powerful enough to sweep down trees.

Flint – a dark-coloured rock. Its hard texture made it ideal to use as an axe-head.

Giant beaver – a bear-sized mammal that was probably better at moving in water than on land. Like the far smaller, modern beaver, it had big teeth for gnawing vegetation.

Giant hyena – a mammal that hunted in packs and probably scavenged because it wasn't built for long chases. It was much larger and less nimble than a hyena today.

Glacier – a huge mass of slow-moving ice.

Ice Age – a long period of time that ended about 20,000 years ago, in which the Earth's temperature cooled and ice sheets and glaciers got bigger.

Permafrost – permanently frozen soil.

Sabre-toothed tiger – a large, heavy-set cat. It had long, sharp canine teeth.

Tundra – a treeless plain where the soil is permanently frozen.

Woolly mammoth – an ancestor of the modern elephant. It had very long, curved tusks. The wool underneath its shaggy hair protected it from the cold.

Other books in the series:

CRETACEOUS

LATE

JURASSIC